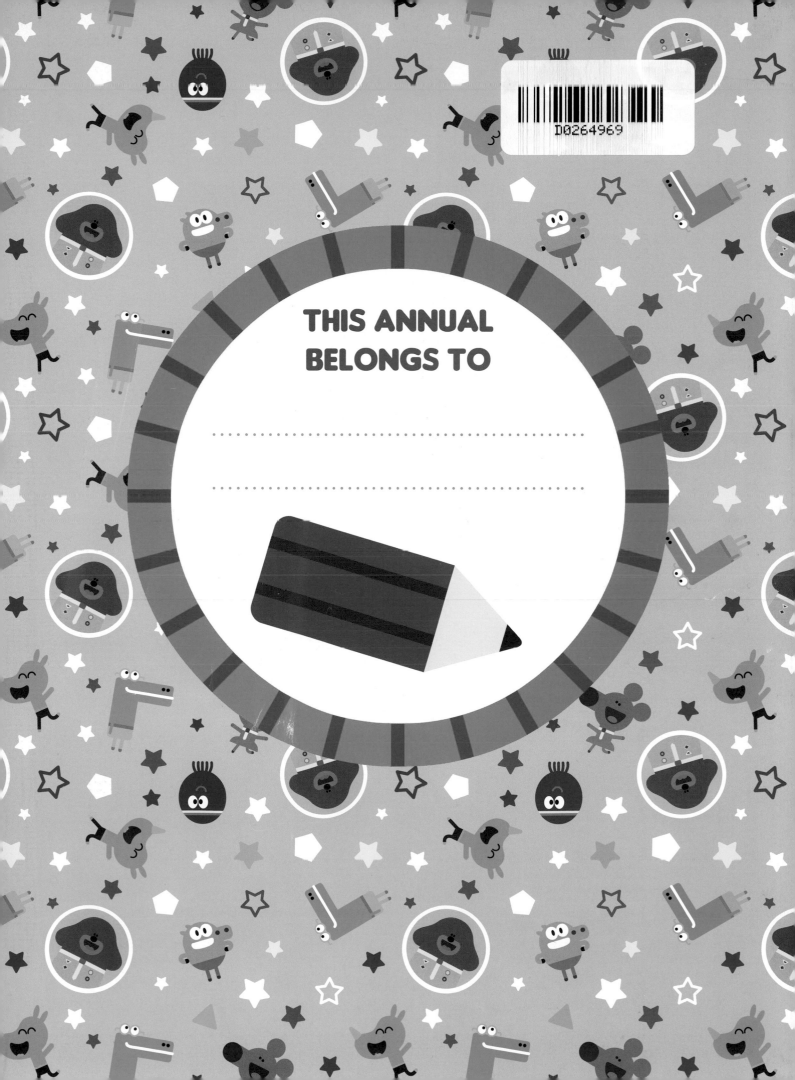

THIS ANNUAL
BELONGS TO

....

....

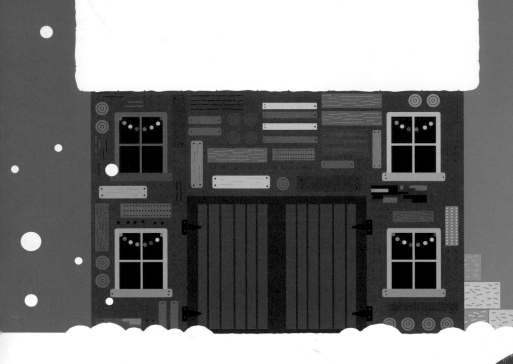

HEY DUGGEE

LADYBIRD BOOKS

UK | USA | Canada | Ireland | Australia | India | New Zealand | South Africa

Ladybird Books is part of the Penguin Random House group of companies
whose addresses can be found at global.penguinrandomhouse.com.

www.penguin.co.uk   www.puffin.co.uk   www.ladybird.co.uk

 Penguin
Random House
UK

First published 2021
002

Text and illustrations copyright © Studio AKA Limited, 2021
Adapted by Jane Kent

Printed in China

The authorized representative in the EEA is Penguin Random House Ireland,
Morrison Chambers, 32 Nassau Street, Dublin D02 YH68

All correspondence to:
Ladybird Books
Penguin Random House Children's
One Embassy Gardens, 8 Viaduct Gardens, London SW11 7BW

DUGGEE

CONTENTS

BETTY

NORRIE

ROLY

TAG

HAPPY

TWINKLE, TWINKLE, LITTLE TREE

Santa Duggee has been decorating the Christmas tree. How many baubles of each colour can you count?

BLUE

ORANGE

PINK

YELLOW

PURPLE

RED

HO! HO! HO!

SNOW MUCH FUN

The Squirrels have been playing in the snow. Which two snow Duggees look exactly the same?

① ② ③ ④ ⑤ ⑥

7

THANK YOU, SANTA!

Santa Duggee has gifts for all the Squirrels.
Use the clues to work out whose
present is whose.

 Roly's gift is wrapped in orange paper.

 Happy's gift is wrapped in purple paper with a green ribbon.

 Norrie's gift has a yellow bow.

 Betty's gift has a purple ribbon.

 Tag's gift has a pink bow.

ANSWERS: Roly – E, Norrie – D, Tag – B, Happy – C, Betty – A

SNOWBALL FIGHT

It's polar bears versus penguins in this great snowball battle! Trace the trails to find out whose snowball hit Duggee. Put a tick by them.

9

DUGGEE DECORATION

Your Christmas tree will look woof-derful with this Angel Duggee decoration on top! Here's how to make it.

YOU WILL NEED

 scissors   glue   A4 card

SCISSORS ARE SHARP! ASK A GROWN-UP FOR HELP.

WHAT TO DO

1. Remove page 11 (or you could photocopy or trace it).

2. Read the labels on page 12 as you will need to remember where the "slots" are for step 4! Glue the picture on to a piece of thin card.

3. Ask a grown-up to help you carefully cut out the picture of Angel Duggee and the wings.

4. Ask a grown-up to help you cut the two slots on Duggee's body and then slot in the wings.

5. Bend the picture into a cone shape and glue the ends together.

6. When the glue is dry, place Angel Duggee on top of your Christmas tree!

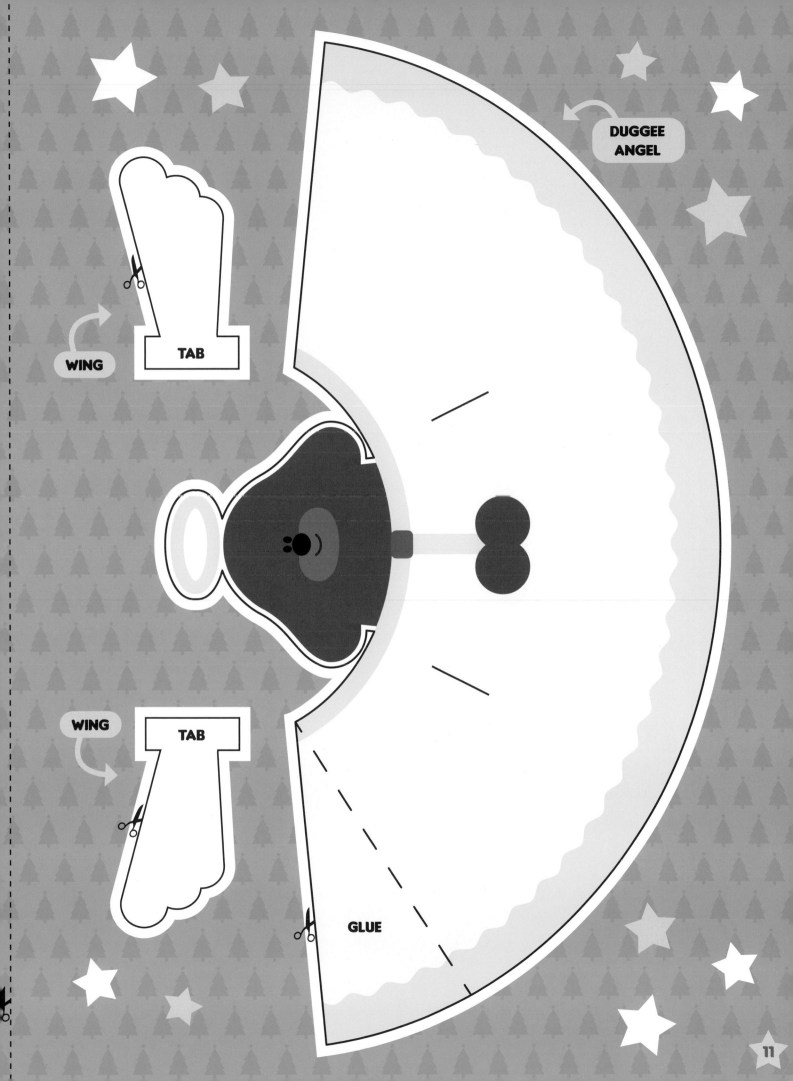

WING

TAB

DUGGEE
ANGEL

WING

TAB

GLUE

11

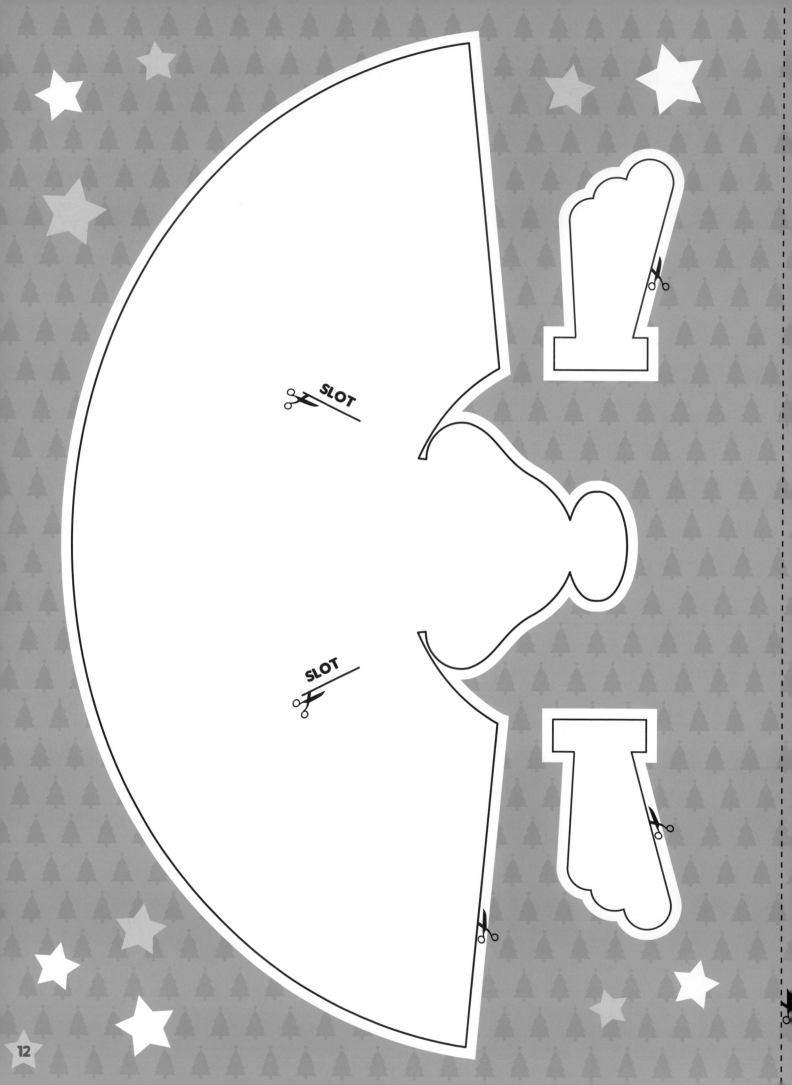

SLOT

SLOT

FESTIVE FIRESIDE

The Squirrels are hanging their Christmas stockings above the fire. Can you answer these questions before Santa arrives to fill them?

1 Who has the biggest stocking?

2 Who has the smallest stocking?

3 Who have stockings that are the same size?

4 Who hasn't hung their stocking on the fireplace yet?

NORRIE

BETTY

TAG

HAPPY

ROLY

13

THE HAIR BADGE

POING!

Duggee is busy combing his hair. He looks in the mirror and smiles. Looking good!

"What are you doing, Duggee?" the Squirrels ask. Duggee flicks the strand of hair. *Poing!* Duggee is having a bad hair day!

Suddenly, more hairs pop up all over Duggee's head. "Ahhhh-woof!" "We'll fix your hair, Duggee!" says Norrie. "How?" asks Happy.

Duggee's got his **Hair Badge!**

"What do we do first, Duggee?" asks Betty. Duggee holds up a bottle of shampoo. First, they must wash his hair.

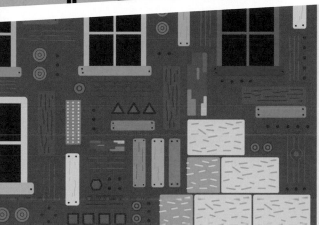

"Yay!" cheer the Squirrels, running outside to find the paddling pool. Duggee comes outside and helps them.

Happy grabs the hose and turns on the tap. "Water!" he cheers.
Roly squirts some shampoo into the water. "BUBBLES!" he shouts.

WATER!

WATER!

BUBBLES!

BUBBLES!

Duggee holds up a paw. That's enough water and bubbles now.
Frog has popped up from the paddling pool in a bubble.

"Wash time, Duggee," says Betty. Duggee climbs into the paddling pool and relaxes.

"Is the water OK, Duggee?" asks Betty.
"Woof!" says Duggee.
"Do you need more bubbles?" asks Roly.
"Woof!" says Duggee, shaking his head.
"Just relax, Duggee," says Norrie.

Duggee starts to shampoo his hair, humming to himself.
"Duggee is washing his hair!" says Norrie.

"Woof!" Duggee has finished washing his hair.
He stands up and shakes himself.
Water splashes everywhere!

Next, the Squirrels must dry Duggee's hair.
"But *how* are we going to do that?" asks Tag.
"I know!" says Happy. He disappears and
comes back with . . .

. . . a giant fan!
"Yay!" cheer the Squirrels.
Happy pushes the button to start the fan.

WHIRRRRRR!

The fan spins faster and faster . . .
"Are you dry yet, Duggee?" shouts Norrie.
"Wooooof!" shouts Duggee, nodding.
Good work, Squirrels.

Happy switches off the fan.
Suddenly, Duggee's hair
puffs up like a giant ball
of fluff.
Duggee looks very funny!

BOOF!

Now the Squirrels must style Duggee's hair.
What style would he like today?

SPIKY HAIR!

BIG HAIR!

CURLY HAIR!

STRAIGHT HAIR!

NO HAIR!

No, that's not right . . . The Squirrels
don't think Duggee suits any of
those hairstyles.

"I've got an idea!" says Tag. He points to a picture of Duggee on the clubhouse wall. The Squirrels whisper together and giggle.

"Finished! We like this one," say the Squirrels. "Woof!" agrees Duggee. It suits you, Duggee!

Hooray! Haven't the Squirrels done well? "Ah-woof!" says Duggee. They have all earned their **Hair Badges**.

Now there's just time for one last thing before the Squirrels go home . . . **"DUGGEE HUG!"**

Well, that was fun, wasn't it, Duggee? Suddenly, Frog's bubble pops and he lands on Duggee's new hair. *Plop!*

RIBBIT!

SUPERSTAR STYLIST

If Duggee was having another bad hair day, what hair style would you give him? Doodle it here to earn your Hair Badge!

POP!

Frog's bubble
is about to pop!
Follow the lines
to find out which
Squirrel's head
he'll land on.

SAY WHAT?

Today Duggee is showing the Squirrels around the farmyard. Draw lines matching each animal to the noise it makes.

BAA!

NEIGH!

CLUCK!

MOO!

ROBO-DUGGEE

The Squirrels have built a robot that looks just like Duggee! Can you find five differences between the two pictures?

23

BEE'S BUSY DAY

Duggee has been teaching the Squirrels all about how honey is made. Follow the bee along the path and answer the questions along the way.

1 Where do bees live?

HIVE

2 What colours are a bee's stripes?

3 Where do bees collect pollen from?

BUZZ!

5 How many bees can you count?

4 What is the leader of the bees called?

FLOWERS

6 What sound do bees make?

QUEEN BEE

B IS FOR BETTY

Betty's name starts with the letter B. Help Betty circle all the things that also start with B.'

ODD DINO OUT

Duggee has travelled back in time to the land of the dinosaurs! In each row, spot the dino that looks different to the others.

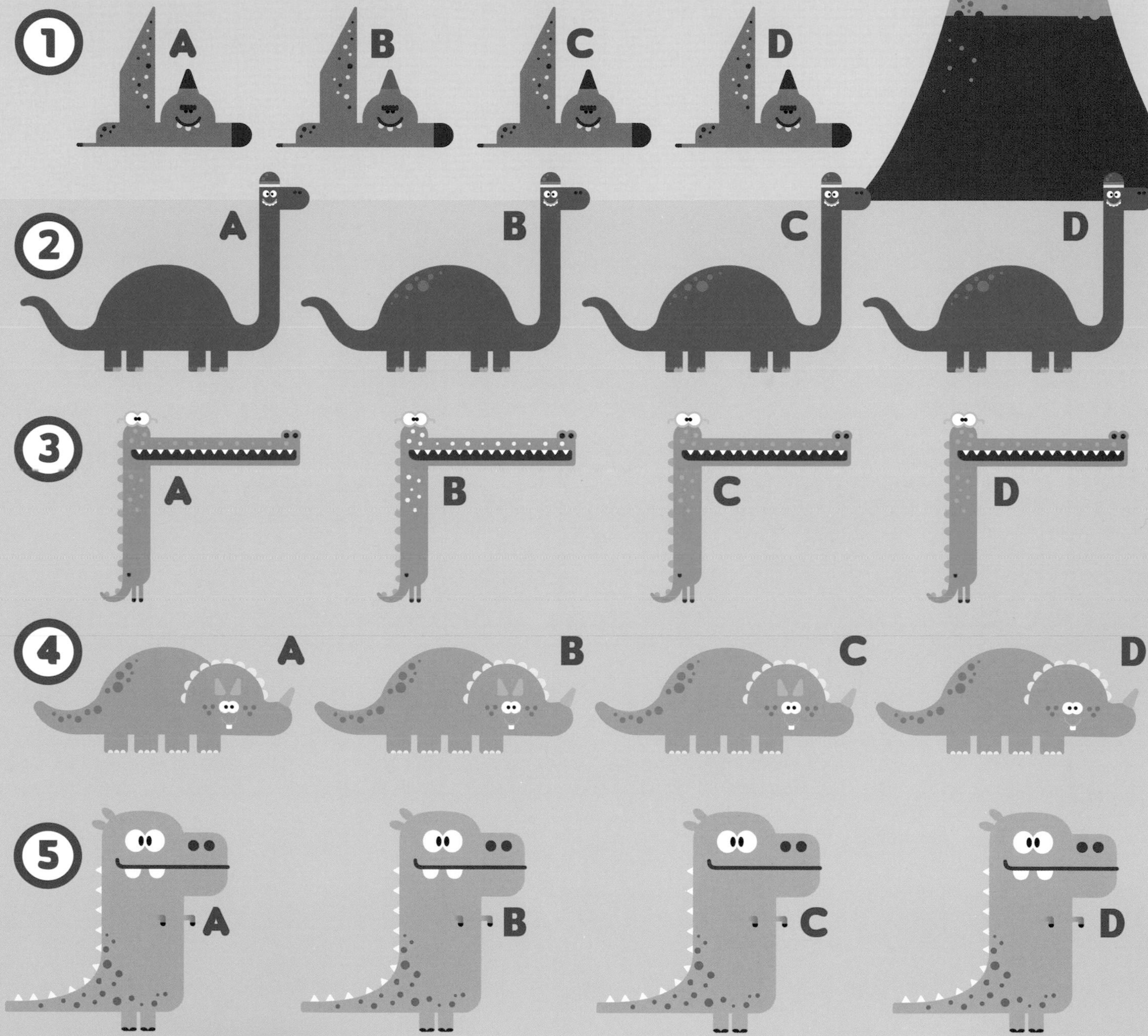

1. A B C D

2. A B C D

3. A B C D

4. A B C D

5. A B C D

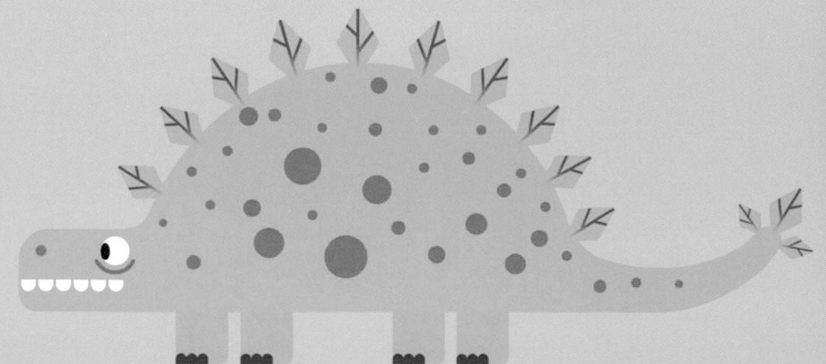

27

PLAYTIME

The Squirrels are playing in the clubhouse. Use the clues to work out which toy they each want to play with.

BOUNCY!

CUDDLES!

LOUD!

GIDDY-UP!

CHOO! CHOO!

ONE, TWO . . . STICK!

Hide-and-Stick is Roly's favourite game.
Help him find the sticks below, hiding
among all the other sticks.

1. THE UPSIDE-DOWN STICK
2. THE SMALLEST STICK
3. THE STICK WITH A MISSING LEAF

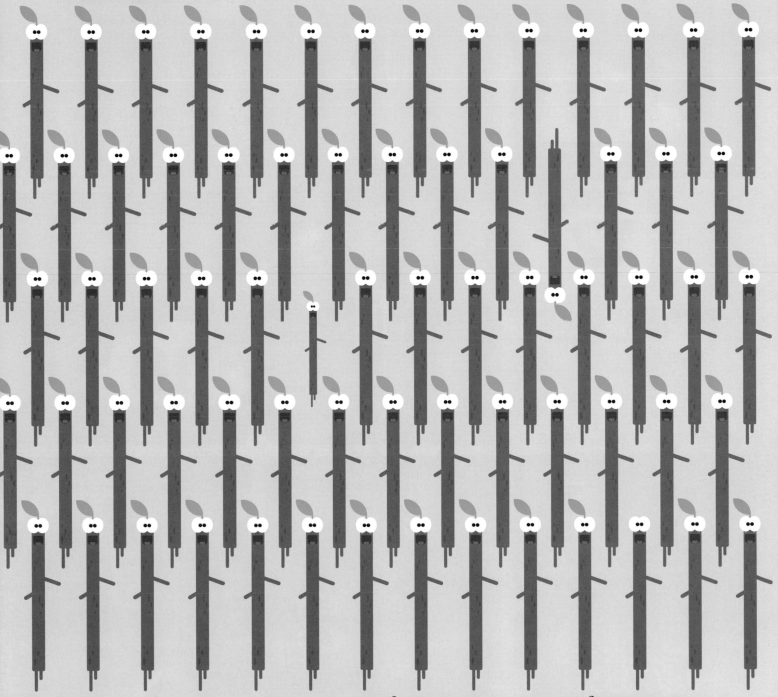

SUNSHINE AND RAINDROPS

This is a great game to play with your pals, whatever the weather!

15

14

13

12

11

10

1

START

2

3

1. Take turns to roll the dice and move your counters round the board. If you land on a grey cloud, follow the raindrops down. If you land on a shining sun, follow the rainbow up.
2. The first player to reach the finish is the winner!

16

17

18
FINISH

9

8

7

4

5

6

31

THE TADPOLE BADGE

It's a lovely sunny morning, and Duggee is outside.
"What are you doing, Duggee?" the Squirrels shout.

Duggee is busy adding the finishing touches to his rock pool.

Happy races towards the rock pool.
"Splashy splash!" he cries.
"Woof!" Duggee holds up his paws.
Sorry, Happy . . . The rock pool isn't for splashing in.

It's for all the animals to enjoy: Duck and her ducklings, the butterflies and Horse.

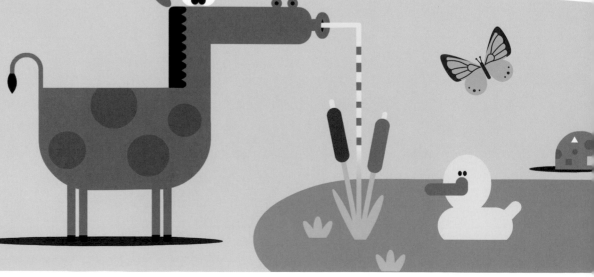

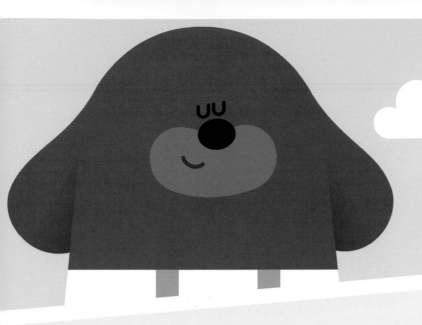

The rock pool is a place of calm, away from the hustle and bustle of everyday life . . .

"What are those?" cries Betty. "Your pond is full of wriggly raisins, Duggee," gasps Norrie.

EURRGHH!

The wriggly raisins are actually babies, and they're called tadpoles.

"Are tadpoles baby worms, Duggee?" asks Betty.
"Baby fish?" asks Happy.
"Baby snails?" asks Norrie.

"Aaaah-woof!" Duggee tells the Squirrels that tadpoles are baby frogs.
"They don't look like Frog," says Tag.
"Or sound like Frog," says Betty.

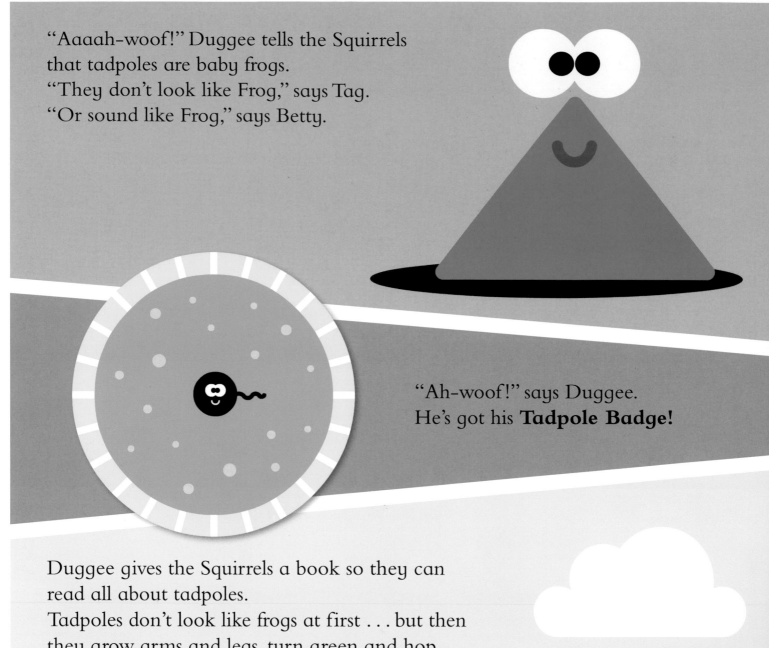

"Ah-woof!" says Duggee.
He's got his **Tadpole Badge!**

Duggee gives the Squirrels a book so they can read all about tadpoles.
Tadpoles don't look like frogs at first . . . but then they grow arms and legs, turn green and hop out of the water as fully-grown frogs.

"That's amazing!" says Betty.
"Do you think they know?" asks Happy.
"Let's tell them," says Tag.

Betty tells the tadpoles what the Squirrels have just found out.
The tadpoles don't like the sound of it.
"No. Way. We're going to stay like this forever!" they shout.

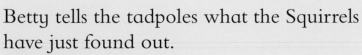

"Arms and legs are disgusting!" cry the tadpoles.
"They're really useful," says Betty.
"He doesn't have legs . . ." say the tadpoles, looking at Frog.
"Yes, he does!" the Squirrels tell them.
Frog stands up and does a little jig.

Suddenly, one tadpole sprouts arm and legs.
Then all of the other tadpoles do too.
"Make it stop!" they cry.
"We can't — it's nature," says Norrie.

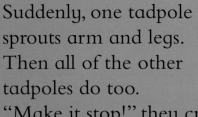
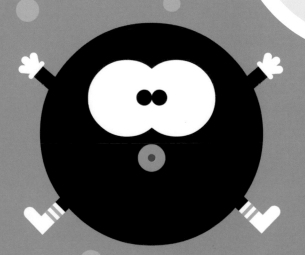

Next the tadpoles turn green and spotty. "Not fair!" they shout.

Finally, the tadpoles turn into frogs.

POP!

"When do they start sounding like Frog?" Tag asks Betty.
She looks in the book. "Er . . . right about now!" she says.
"I'm never going to sound like . . . RIBBIT!" one little frog croaks.
All the little frogs start to ribbit.

RIBBIT!

The frogs begin to leave the pond.
"Hey, where are you going?" asks Tag.

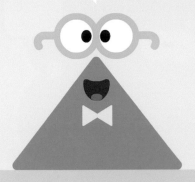

TO STUDY!

TO WORK IN THE CITY!

TO GO TRAVELLING!

"Wow! They grow up so fast," says Tag.
"Bye-bye, tadpoles . . . I mean, frogs!"
calls Betty sadly.

Hooray! Haven't the
Squirrels done well?
"Ah-woof!" says Duggee.
They have all earned
their **Tadpole Badges**.

Now there's just time for
one last thing before the
Squirrels go home . . .

"DUGGEE HUG!"

RIBBIT!

Betty loved finding out about frogs from Duggee's book. Help her put these pictures in order, from a tiny tadpole to a fully-grown frog.

ANSWERS: A.2, B.3, C.4, D.1

A HOPPY HOME

Duggee thinks these frogs are ready to leave the rock pool. Match each frog to their shadow before they hop off into the big wide world.

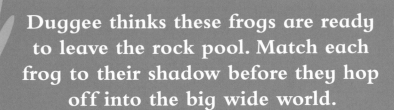

1  **A**  **B**  **C**

2  **A**  **B**  **C**

3  **A**  **B**  **C**

4  **A**  **B**  **C**

THE MEMORY GAME

You and a friend can join Duggee for some badge-collecting fun!

HOW TO PLAY

1. Ask a grown-up to help you carefully cut out the badges.

2. Shuffle the badges and turn them all over so they are face down.

3. Take turns to flip over two badges. If they match, keep the badges and tick off the badge on your scorecard. If the badges don't match, turn them back over.

4. When all of the badges have been matched, the player with the most badges ticked off on their scorecard wins!

PLAYER 1

PLAYER 2

DO THE FUNKY CHICKEN

Duggee is an egg-cellent dancer, but he's keen to learn some cracking new moves! Join him by copying the chickens' peck-peck poses.

YOU WILL NEED

 a dice a dance partner (optional)

HOW TO PLAY

1. Roll the dice.
2. Every number on the dice matches a dance move. Put on your favourite song and try out the move you rolled!
3. Roll again. Which move will you perform next?
4. Continue until you're tired from dancing!

STEP TO THE RIGHT

STEP TO THE LEFT

SHOUT "CLUCK CLUCK!"

GIVE A THUMBS UP

TOUCH YOUR TOES

STAND ON ONE LEG

READY, SET, GROW!

The Squirrels have grown sunflowers in the clubhouse garden. Put them in height order from the shortest to the tallest.

SHORTEST ▢ ▢ ▢ ▢ ▢ TALLEST

44

DUGGEE DOOR HANGER

Make your bedroom into your very own clubhouse by hanging this sign on the door.

 crayons or colouring pencils scissors glue A4 card

YOU WILL NEED

WHAT TO DO

 SCISSORS ARE SHARP! ASK A GROWN-UP FOR HELP.

1. Remove page 47 (or you could photocopy it).

2. Colour in the door hanger.

3. Add glue to the back of the hanger and stick it on to a piece of thin card.

4. Fold the hanger in half along the dotted lines, and glue the halves together.

5. Ask a grown-up to help you cut out the hanger.

6. Hang it from the doorknob of your clubhouse!

COME IN AND EARN SOME BADGES!

COME IN AND EARN SOME BADGES!

KEEP OUT! SQUIRRELS SLEEPING!

SPLASHY SPLASH

Happy is leading the Squirrels on a splash-tastic adventure! Help him find a path to Duggee by jumping only in the puddles with the letter D.

THE RIVER BADGE

Duggee needs to deliver a very special parcel.

He points to a spot on a map.
"At the end of that blue road?" asks Tag.
The blue road is actually a river.

"But you can't swim that far . . ." says Betty.
Duggee puts on his captain's hat and points to the badge on the front of it. Duggee's got his **River Badge!**

PAAAARP!

Soon Duggee and his crew are ready to set sail.
"Ah-woof!"
Roly toots the boat's horn, and off they go . . .

Duggee and the Squirrels are having a great time sailing down the river. "Hello, Chicken!" calls Tag.

SQWARK!

Betty is busy checking their course on the map. They're on the right route!

Roly spots a little cord hanging down from his life jacket. He pulls it . . .

Norrie is putting the life rings in their proper place, making them nice and neat.

Happy points ahead. "WATER!" he shouts.
"Yes, Happy," says Betty, nodding.
"WATER!" Happy shouts again.
"We know it's water, Happy!" says Betty.
"WATER . . . BUFFALO!" shouts Happy.
"Huh?" says Betty. "DUGGEE!"

"WOOF!" Duggee
spins the wheel. The
boat swerves and
misses the water
buffalo.
"Phew!" cry the
Squirrels.

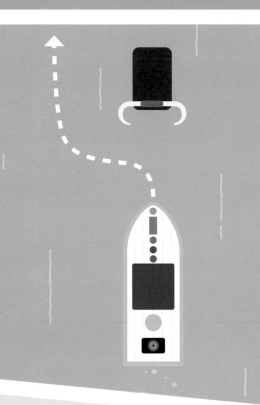

"DUCK-BILLED PLATYPUS!"
shouts Tag.
"WOOF!" Duggee spins the
wheel again. The boat swerves.
"Phew!" cry the Squirrels as
they sail safely past the
duck-billed platypus.

"WATER . . . FALL!"
shouts Happy.
"Woooooof!"
Hold on tight, Squirrels!

The boat sails over the
waterfall, and then bounces
through some rapids.
The Squirrels giggle. "Yay!"

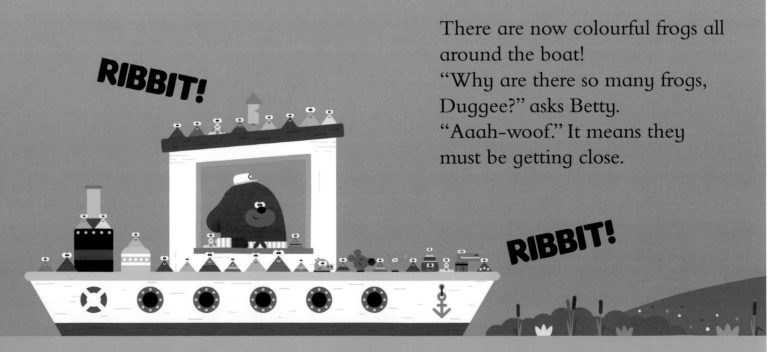

RIBBIT!

RIBBIT!

There are now colourful frogs all
around the boat!
"Why are there so many frogs,
Duggee?" asks Betty.
"Aaah-woof." It means they
must be getting close.

Duggee tells Roly that it's time to toot the boat's horn again.
POP! Suddenly, a rabbit appears on the riverbank.
"Hey, man. You've brought the parcel, yeah?" he asks.
Duggee nods. "Woof."

"Watch out, man, it can be a bit slippy-dippy," the rabbit tells them.
The Squirrels carefully climb out of the boat.

As Duggee climbs out, he slips and falls into the river.

WOOF!

"She's in there, man," the rabbit says, pointing to a temple.
The Squirrels follow Duggee inside. "Hellooooo!" they call.

They hear a voice in the darkness. "Hello, sweetlings . . ." It's Chew Chew!

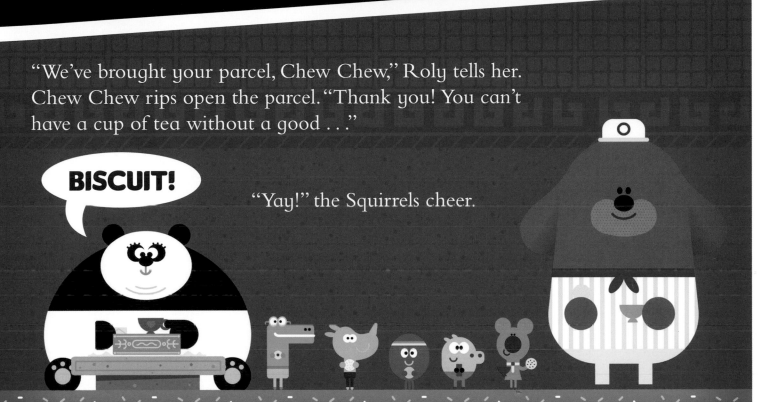

"We've brought your parcel, Chew Chew," Roly tells her. Chew Chew rips open the parcel. "Thank you! You can't have a cup of tea without a good . . ."

BISCUIT!

"Yay!" the Squirrels cheer.

Hooray! Haven't the Squirrels done well? "Ah-woof!" says Duggee. They have all earned their **River Badges**. Before they set sail for home, there's just time for one more thing . . .

"DUGGEE HUG!"

HUNGRY PANDA

Chew Chew LOVES biscuits! Which box has she taken one from, to eat with her cup of tea?

1

2

3

ANSWER: Chew Chew has taken a biscuit from box 2.

HIDE-AND-HOP

Happy is playing a fun game with his hoppy new friends. Help him find the six frogs hiding in the scene.

SWIMMING SEQUENCES

Happy has found some feathered friends who love to splash around in the water too! Work out which little duckling comes next in each row.

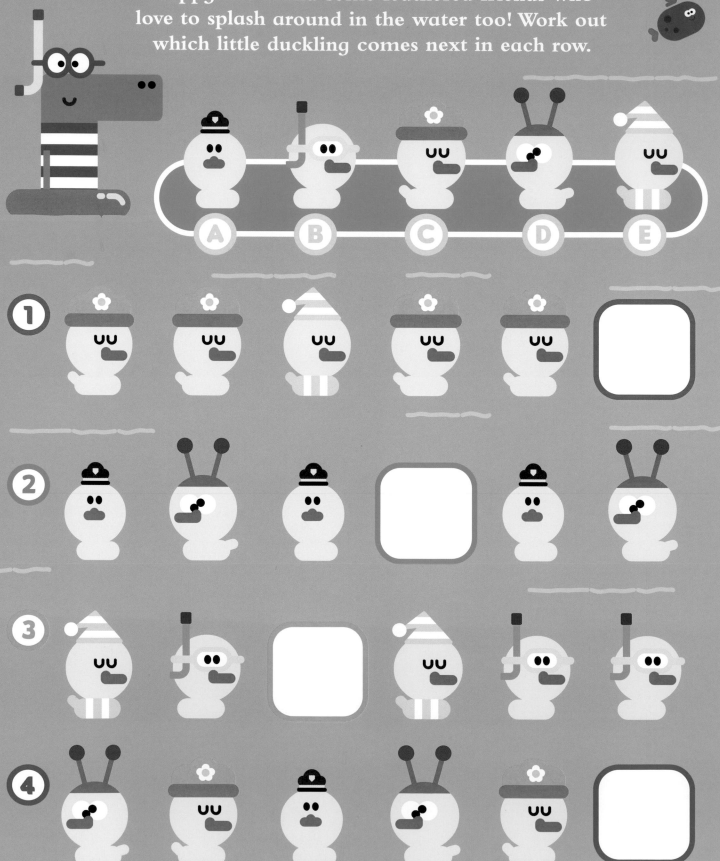

YUMMY CUPCAKES

Chef Duggee has been baking treats for
the Squirrels. Draw lines to link these
pretty cupcakes into pairs.

CHOO! CHOO!

Today Duggee is taking the Squirrels on a train ride. Complete the picture by matching the jigsaw pieces to the right spaces.

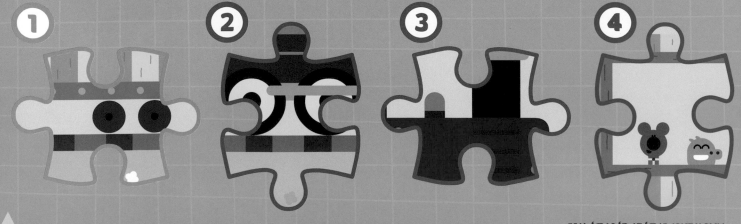

60

TIME FOR FUN!

Duggee and the Squirrels always fill their days with adventures. Trace the hands of the clocks to show what time they will do each fun activity.

It's ten o'clock – time for a day out!

It's two o'clock – time to build a sandcastle!

It's four o'clock – time to have a dance party!

HEY DUGGEE

LOOK OUT FOR THESE OTHER GREAT HEY DUGGEE BOOKS!

PICTURE BOOKS

HEY DUGGEE DUGGEE AND THE STICK BADGE

DUGGEE AND THE CHRISTMAS BADGE

HEY DUGGEE DUGGEE AND THE DINOSAURS

HEY DUGGEE SUPER DUGGEE

HEY DUGGEE TREASURE HUNT

A LIFT-THE-FLAP BOOK

HEY DUGGEE DUGGEE AND THE SQUIRRELS

HEY DUGGEE BUGGY BOOK

NOVELTY

HEY DUGGEE THE POTTY BADGE

HEY DUGGEE THE FOOTBALL BADGE

STICKER ACTIVITY

HEY DUGGEE SUMMER STICKER ACTIVITY BOOK

BOARD BOOKS

HEY DUGGEE DUGGEE'S CHRISTMAS